KITTEN

Pickle

Lynne Dennis

Carnival

Pickle the kitten wakes up.
She wants to play.

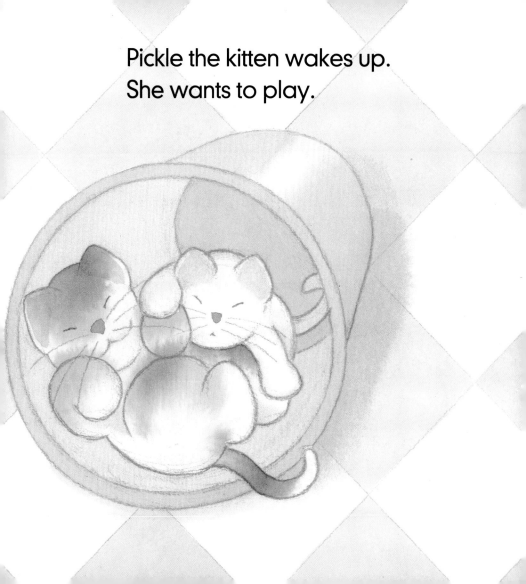

She climbs out of the toy box.
Hop and Scotch want to play too.

Pickle steps on Snowflake's tail.
"Miaow!" says Snowflake.

Hop and Scotch tip up the toy box.
Crash! Snooze wakes up.

Pickle goes for a ride on the car.

Bump! The car hits the bricks.
Pickle falls off. She walks away
with her tail in the air.
"Come and see this mouse,
Pickle," says Snooze.

Whizz! The mouse runs
away from Snooze.
Pickle runs after the mouse.
She stops it with her paws.

"I'm going to play with the train now," says Pickle.
She climbs on top of it.

Hop and Scotch bump into the train.
It starts to move.

Off goes Pickle. Snowflake, Snooze,
Hop and Scotch run after her.

The train slows down and the kittens catch up with Pickle.
"I'm sleepy now," says Pickle. "It's time for a nap."